DUCK SOUP

Jackie Urbanovic

SCHOLASTIC INC.
New York Toronto London Auckland
Sydney Mexico City New Delhi Hong Kong

ISBN 978-0-545-25560-8

Copyright © 2008 by Jackie Urbanovic. All rights reserved. Published by Scholastic Inc., 557 Broadway, New York, NY 10012, by arrangement with HarperCollins Children's Books, a division of HarperCollins Publishers. SCHOLASTIC and associated logos are trademarks and/or registered trademarks of Scholastic Inc.

12 11 10 9 8 7 6 5 4 3 2   10 11 12 13 14 15/0

Printed in the U.S.A.   40

First Scholastic printing, March 2010

Typography by Carla Weise

To Marcia for *everything*, especially the past ten years of generous advice and conversation.

Special acknowledgment to the Marx Brothers for "borrowing" their movie title.

This was it!

A little pepper, some salt, a little parsley and potato—SOUP! This would be Max's masterpiece.

"OOOOOOO-LA-LA!

This is going to be grand."

Max had made lots of soups before—

Fish Soup with Curry
and Pickled Lemon,

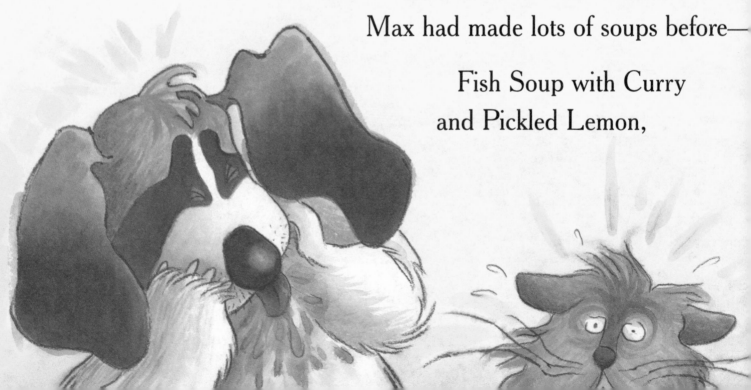

Red HOT Chili Soup,
Squash Gumbo,

Cracker Barrel Cheese and
Marshmallow Soup, and Way,
Way Too Many Beans Soup.

He had cooked them all!
But every recipe had been created
by another chef, not Max.

Now he was making his own soup.

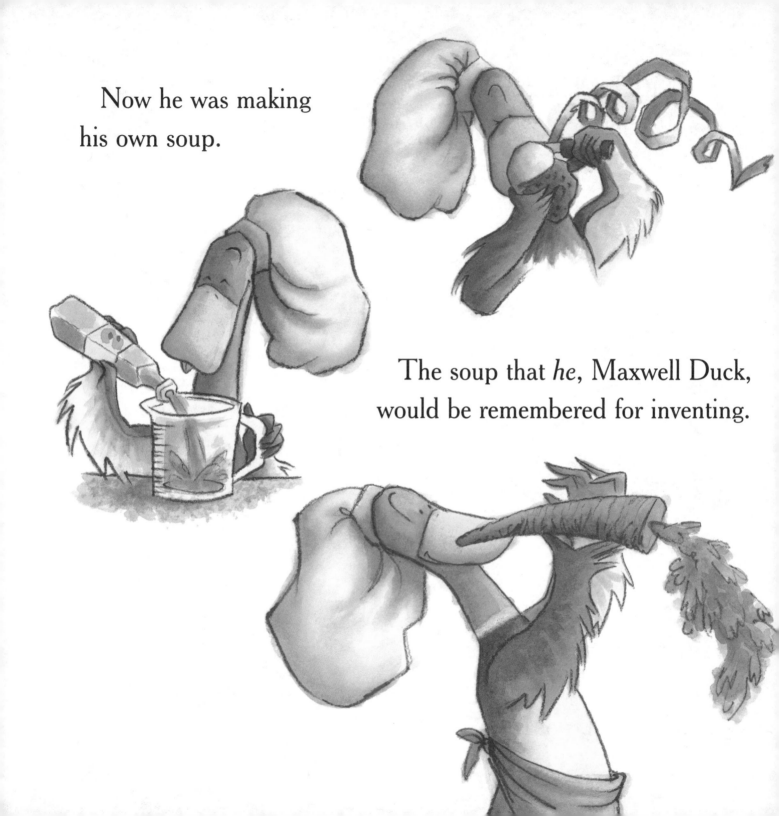

The soup that *he*, Maxwell Duck, would be remembered for inventing.

"It needs an herb from the garden! Just wait, my delicate broth. Max will be back to make you *perfecto* in *uno momento*!"

SMACK! The front door slammed shut as Brody, Dakota, and Bebe walked in.

SNIFF
SNIFF

"Ooh! What smells so good?" asked Brody.

"Max must be cooking again. I hope it's better than last time!" said Dakota.

Hey, Max! Maxie!

"Where are yoooooouuuuu?" called Brody.
"We're about to eat your soup!" added Dakota.

"So—what's wrong?" asked Brody.
"Taste it, already, Dakota!"

Dakota gasped. "I think I know where Max went."

"Call for help!" cried Bebe.

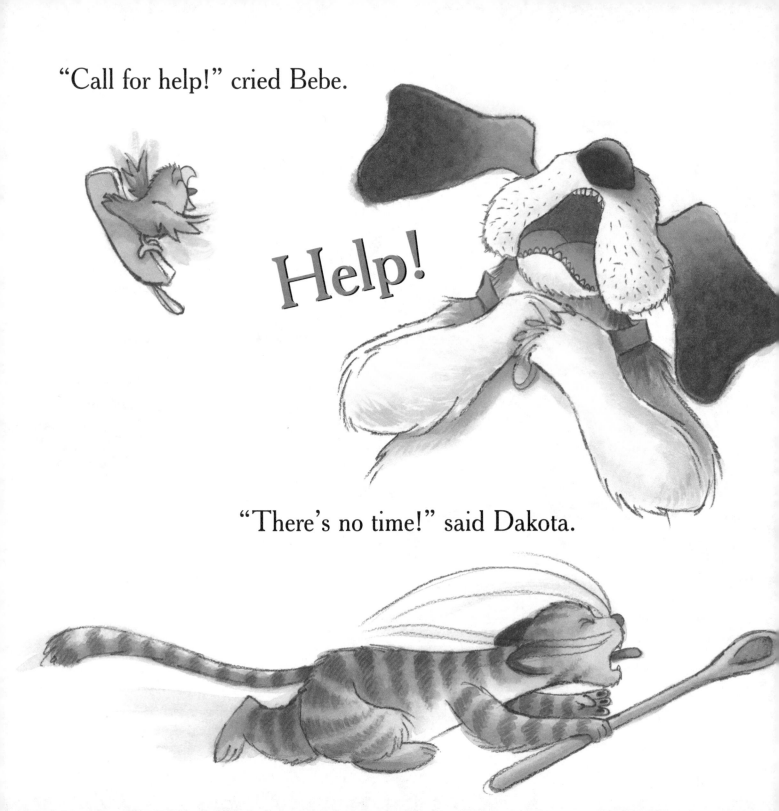

Help!

"There's no time!" said Dakota.

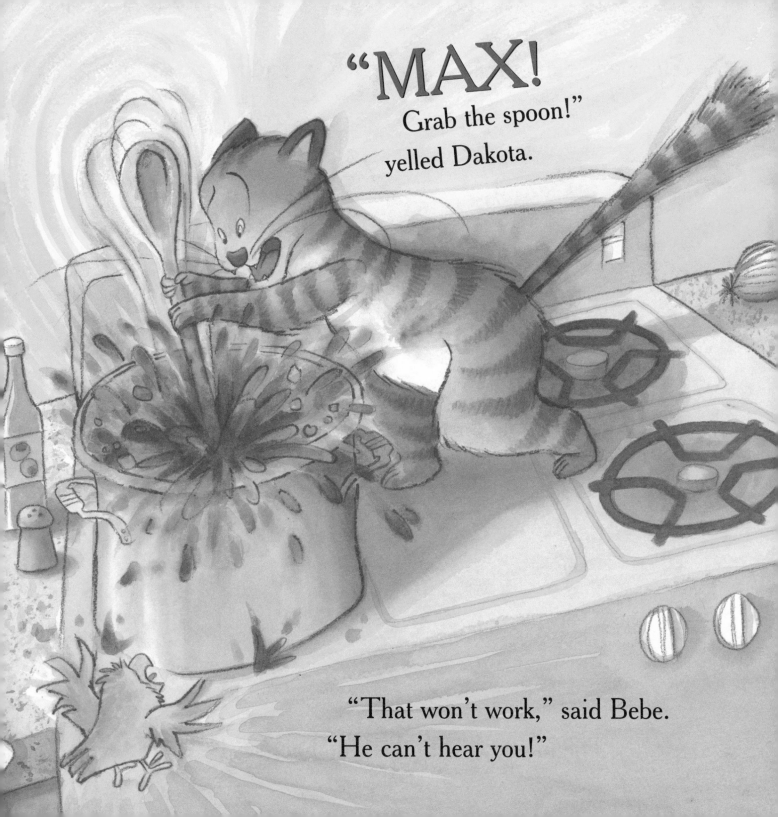

"I KNOW! THE STRAINER!"

"Strainer?"

"The big bowl with the little holes! GRAB IT!"

Brody hoped that the soup
would go down the drain and
Max would stay behind.

"AHHHHH!
It's his head!" said Bebe.

"Silly! It's only a potato!"
Brody replied.

"EYEBALLS!

His eyeballs!" said Bebe.

"Guys, it's only tiny onions!" said Brody.

"HIS FEET!" yelled Dakota.

"Calm down, you two! It's only carrot slices!" said Brody.

SMACK!

They all looked up as the
front door slammed shut.
Who could that be?

That night Max was very quiet over dinner.

"Cheer up, Max. You're still a great chef," said Irene.

"And you'll cook your perfect soup someday soon," she added.

"And it'll be great!" said Brody.

"Really great!" said Bebe.

"We know you're disappointed," said Irene.
"But at least you're not duck soup."

And they all agreed.
EVEN Max.